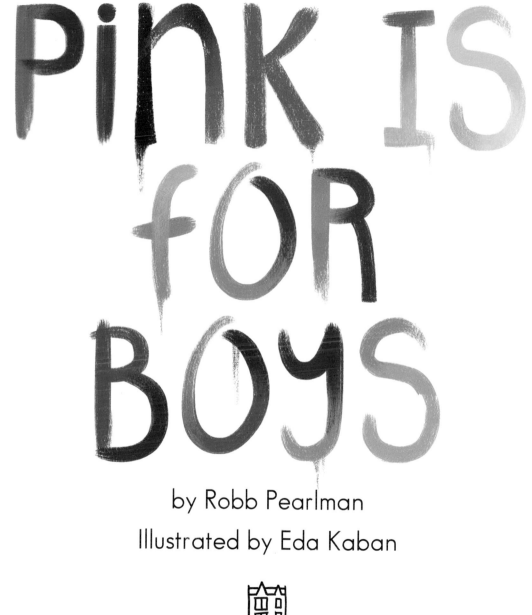

PINK IS FOR BOYS

by Robb Pearlman

Illustrated by Eda Kaban

RP | KIDS
PHILADELPHIA

Running Press Kids
Hachette Book Group
1290 Avenue of the Americas, New York, NY 10104
www.runningpress.com/rpkids
@RP_Kids

Printed in China

First Edition: June 2018

Published by Running Press Kids, an imprint of Perseus Books, LLC,
a subsidiary of Hachette Book Group, Inc.

The Hachette Speakers Bureau provides a wide range of authors for speaking events.
To find out more, go to www.hachettespeakersbureau.com or call (866) 376-6591.

The publisher is not responsible for websites (or their content)
that are not owned by the publisher.

Print book cover and interior design by Frances J. Soo Ping Chow

Library of Congress Control Number: 2017933537

ISBNs: 978-0-7624-6247-6 (hardcover), 978-0-7624-6248-3 (ebook),
978-0-7624-9211-4 (ebook), 978-0-7624-9212-1 (ebook)

1010

10 9 8 7 6 5 4 3 2 1

THIS BOOK, AND EVERY COLOR,
IS FOR MOZE.

—R. P.

THIS BOOK IS FOR MOM,
THE MOST COLORFUL PERSON I KNOW

—E. K.

PINK is for boys.
And girls.

And bows
on fancy clothes.

BLUE is for girls.
And boys.

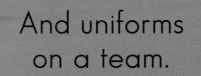

And uniforms
on a team.

YELLOW is for boys.
And girls.

And a crown
to wear.

GREEN is for girls.
And boys.

And grass
to run on.

RED is for boys.
And girls.

And cars
racing along the track.

ORANGE is for girls.
And boys.

And popsicles
dribbling down sticky chins.

PURPLE is for boys.
And girls.

And unicorns,
because . . . unicorns!

BROWN is for girls.
And boys.

And teddy bears
to cuddle.

BLACK and WHITE are for boys and girls.
And puppies and kittens
to pet.

And all the colors are for **EVERYONE**.
Girls and boys.

And flowers.
And butterflies.
And rainbows
in the sky.